TALES AND POEMS FOR EVERYONE

COLLECTION OF SHORT STORIES AND POEMS

BY

LAKSHMI BEMPLASSERI

ISBN 978-93-5438-100-3

Published in India 2020 by Pencil

A brand of
One Point Six Technologies Pvt. Ltd.
123, Building J2, Shram Seva Premises,
Wadala Truck Terminal, Wadala (E)
Mumbai 400037, Maharashtra, INDIA
E connect@thepencilapp.com
W www.thepencilapp.com

Author biography

Hi Readers...I am a retired college Professor and I have M Sc M Phil in Chemistry. I am married and I have two children who have Ph D in English and Chemistry respectively. My interests include reading and occasionally jotting down a short piece related to my current circumstances. I have published only in our college magazine....five or six short stories, which I thought I will reproduce here in book form. Hoping they give you a few minutes of enjoyment.

Contents

A High Tech Pret 06

The Mouse in the House 13

Shades 16

The Ill Behav 18

My Rain 21

Relaaax…Zzz…Ing 23

Stop Dyeing and Start Living 26

A Lazy Midsummer Afternoon—
A Rare Communion 28

The Birthing 32

A HIGH TECH PRET

(This story is dedicated to my two kids who have acquired mobile phones lately. The germ of the story is theirs—I only fleshed it out. I also acknowledge their technical help. I....er...um...don't own a cell phone)

The time was nearly 6'o clock.It was still dark outside.

'klim'.....the sound of a message dropping into her mobile phone could pull her out of even the deepest sleep. "Who the hell is thinkng of me at such an unearthly hour?" She was barely awake. "Must be one of those larks who keep ungodly hours and expect others to do so". She opened her inbox. "Happy Birthday Subbu". "Ha!so u remembered after all". Everyone else had wished her on the stroke of midnight and she had sat up until nearly two planning the details of the birthday bash with them.When she lay down again there was a smile on her lips. Seventeen...sweet seventeen..she mused...the passport to the adult world (you have to wait till you are eighteen for the visa...but that was OK). Then there was the party –just she and her friends---the new dress—Oh !—life was good indeed! The mobile alarm woke her at 7. She lay enjoying the song for a few minutes then switched off the alarm.Immediately her dialer tune commenced—her favourite song. (she had fallen in love with it the moment she had heard it on Star Singer....Nizhalaay ....ozhukivarum njaan.....) With that began her daily ritual of exchanging "Good Morning" with her friends. Suddenly she remembered…she had'nt told her mother about her birthday party and that she did'nt want lunch. She immediately speed dialed Mom. "Good morning mom. I forgot to tell u yesterday –I'm giving a party to my friends today afternoon. So I don't want lunch today" " U could have told me yesterday. It would have saved a lot of trouble" "Oh mom I forgot.Mo..om ..but u did'nt wish me happy birthday" "Happy birthday dear. Enjoy yourself" "Thank u mom" She cut the call and immediately the mobile started ringng. She walked with it to the bathroom.

Meet one of the Subhashini's of the 2k era (that's yr 2 kilo…i.e the 2000's)---loquatious on the phone or on the SMS—but cannot utter a word without the phone in her ear.She needs the mobile to talk even to her mom and dad—at the very least a hand to her ear if she has to utter a word.

By and by Subbu is dressed and ready for college in her new birthday outfit (Cheee not birthday suit and don't ask me what she is wearing. Suffice to say it's the latest in fashion.You can refer "What the fashionable teenager wears" written by Mr. Sumbdy Orather.)

She eats a skechy breakfast and bolts out the door late as usual with the phone in her ear. She has to take two buses to college and from the town stop the buses are rather few. So she walks quickly to the bus stop. Suddenly she sees her bus coming. She has to cross the road to the bus stop. With the phone still in her ear and her eye on the bus she crosses the road and walks straight into a pot hole, loses her balance and falls in the middle of the road. Her phone is thrown from her hand and as she watches horrified, a car ....Subbu closes her eyes tight and puts her hands to her ears, but could not cut off the sickening scrunch of the tyres. An agony so intense sweeps through her as though the car had passed right over her. The intense pain makes her cry out and then mercifully she faints.

When she comes to, she finds she has been moved to the side of the road and there is a crowd gathered. She gets up shakily and looks toward her ruined mobile. Now the agony she feels is like a knife in her side. It was like losing a hand or leg—it had been so much a part of her. She walks towards the mobile and picks it up. Completely gone. She takes out the sim card. Can she use it again? Well she would ask the dealer when she bought the new mobile. She puts the sim in her bag. It was then that the real immensity of her situation hit her. She was phoneless!!!and all her friends' phone numbers and all their details were here in this ruined sim card, She did not know any phone numbers not even that of her home or her dad's. Where could she get the money for a new phone? She surely couldn't go to college without a phone. It was unthinkable!!!She stood there not knowing what to do. Finally she decided to go home and ask her mom for the cash. She took an auto home.

Her mom was worried when she saw her disheveled daughter coming in at the gate as she looked out through the window. She hastily opened the door. "What happened dear? You look quite ill." "I fell down on the road" she said with difficulty. "I have to buy new phone and I don't have any money."She dissolved into tears. She cried on her mother's shoulder till she was spent and felt slightly better. "Mom I just must buy a new phone immediately. I can't go to college without a mobile—and that too on my birthday!" "All right dear. I have only 5000/- with me now. I'll give you that." "W..ell, I suppose I'll have to make do with that" There goes my microwave--her mother laments silently to herself.

Finally Subbu is off once more with the money her mother gave her and after making the necessary repairs to her appearance. She manages to land an identical phone as the one she lost. There was a sale—and it was a 5 year old model—so they were giving it off at a discount. Her old sim which she had salvaged from the shattered mobile was useless. She had to buy a new sim.She fed as many of her lost contacts and messages as she could from her friends' mobiles and that almost restored her mood. So that she enjoyed her birthday bash after all.

As the days passed however, a slow change seemed to come over her. Outwardly nothing had changed. She was still the same mobile maniac—talking nineteen to the dozen on her mobile, sending SMS—in short glued to her mobile every minute of the day. But inwardly she was becoming aware that something untoward was going on. Once or twice, just as she was dropping off to sleep, she thought she heard the ring tone of her old mobile. She was too sleepy to bother to pick up her mobile and thought she must have imagined it. It was too faint to make out clearly,anyhow.And once she had heard the "klim" sound of a message. But when she had opened the message it was a blank. And the number from which the message was sent wasn't displayed. It got so bad that she stared losing sleep and appetite and began to look quite wan and listless.

Her mother sensed the change in her and tried her best to lure her out of her apathy by cooking her favorite dishes and arranging outings. But nothing seemed to work. And then, one day, as she was about to cross the road at the place where the accident had occurred, she heard the ring tone of her old mobile quite clearly—Nizhalaay.... ozhukivarum njaan.She hastily took out her mobile. New call. She looked at the caller ID—9934658198—her old number. A bolt of lightning seemed to shoot from her toes to the top of her head. She could not move. She stood there staring at the display, her eyes bulging out of her head. Without thinking she pushed the call button and put the mobile to her ear. "The IDEA number you are calling has ceased to exist". As she put the phone back in her bag and ran pell-mell down the road the haunting melody seemed to pursue her all the way to the college.

That night she couldn't sleep. She was scared to be alone in her own room for the first time in her life. She resolutely lay down on the bed covered herself with the shawl and closed her eyes determined to sleep. But sleep wouldn't come. She remembered a line from some poem her teacher had read out once—'Fear at my heart as at a cup my life blood seemed to sip' It had caught her imagination then. Little did she know that she would one day fall into the same predicament? Was it presentiment that had attracted her to the ancient mariner?'Klim' Oh how she had come to hate that sound. But pick up she must—her body and mind refused to obey her anymore. She picked up the phone—what was the use of the tug of war?she always lost in the end.It was a voice SMS.She opened the message. "Aaaahhh......" a cry of pure agony rent the silence to shreds.She dropped the phone on the bed.She could'nt even cry out—the terrible fear had her by the throat.For she had recognized the cry—hers—the moment the car had run down her mobile!

The next day she resolved to get rid of her mobile first thing in the morning. "And the old sim," she told herself. "Maybe that was what was causing all the problems." The decision seemed to calm her, so that, she was able to eat a decent breakfast. She decided to throw it into the river near her collge.She crossed the road quickly to the town bus stop(the site of the accident) eager to be rid of the terrible burden. She had reached the middle of the road when 'Nizhalaay.....' followed by the agonizing cry. She stopped in the middle of the road frantically trying to pull the mobile out of her bag and throw it away. The car was coming at a good speed. The driver had expected her to cross the road and not stop right in the middle. There was no time to change course. An instant---and then ----- the essence that was Subbu was spread out and scattered over the whole universe like the shock waves spreading out from a nuclear bomb.

How long did it take to reassemble?A minute?a month ?a year?who knows?But finally she opened her eyes and sat up.She still had the mobile phone in her hand.Her old mobile. A strange smile spread over her lips. She punched in a number and pressed the call button and put the phone to her ear. The strange smile still played about her lips.

THE MOUSE IN THE HOUSE

THE MOUSE IN THE HOUSE

Thud...thud...thud...coming from the tiny tin loft above my kitchen sink-work space. It must be 7.30-8 in the evening, the TV blaring full blast with back-to-back serials...almost all of them featuring lachrymose women and cherubic children being subjected to a variety of tortures and, of course, the Ammayiamma, whose terrible visage would give you nightmares. So very much removed from real life.

Well...where was I?..Aahh..the mouse. It's not the first one to get into the house. Though how it does get in we have never been able to determine exactly. So off I go to break the news gently to my husband who's in front of the TV.

"There's another mouse in the loft"

"What?" ...he's too caught up in the drama on TV... something very momentous is happening. It was really bad timing. Well! Can't be helped. So I repeat "I just heard thuds from the loft. It must be another mouse."

"Oh! Will it never stop? I must have killed at least a 100 mice. How many times have I told you not to keep the windows open? You light the lamp and pray to Krishna and then you make me do all these sins. Don't think you are going to escape the consequences yourself."

What was that? It was a new one indeed! I hadn't opened any windows this time. The work area has a tiled roof instead of RC. The mice could very well be coming in through an unnoticed gap in the tiles. But no! the fault's always mine and the mice can come in only through an open window. One day, who knows, the mice may ring the bell andwait on the doorstep, and push past me as I open the door. Huh! The last remark got me so riled I gave him he silent treatment for all of 3 hours.

But then I thought-you can't blame him. Catching the mouse is his job—and killing it and disposing of the body too. Ugh!

Well, the whole rigmarole of baiting the trap, keeping it on the loft, and waiting for the mouse to walk in and get caught. Usually it works very well. We, maybe, have to change the bait a time or two. But this one refused to bite.

Then one night, as I came down after lights out, lighting my way with my mobile torch, ther it was-THE MOUSE-a tiny one hardly bigger than a lizard. It had managed to come inside from the work area it now had easy access to all rooms including the bedrooms. At least in the work area it could be isolated by closing the door. Disaster indeed!

At sight of me the mouse scampered around the room finally jumping into the store room. Thank God! It was another isolation zone. I jumped just as fast and secured the door before it could get out. I switched on the store room light and slowly opened the door a crakk and dragged out the bucket containing rice and a the bottles congaing the bare essentials required for the next day and again closed the door tight.

Then we set the trap in the store room. But the mouse was clever-it ate the bait but didn't get caught. In effect we were feeding it like a pet. Finally there was no other go but to use the last resort-poison. And after leading us a merry dance it was finally caught. May its soul, the souls all previously killed mice, and the souls all mice to be killed in future find peace and a better life in the next birth.

SHADES

SHADES

Shades!...........seen only through the corner of ones eyes heard only at the very edge of ones consciousness.... disappearing entirely ....or....morphing into some everyday object or sound when focused upon.....shades!!!

Like.....when I sit engrossed in the late night movie, the dinner dishes forgotten, lateness of the hour forgotten.... and at last, with tears still wet on my cheeks at the poignant ending, when I stand beside the sink to finish the inevitable chore, when everybody else is in bed and snoring, and the house itself is settling down for the night with eerie creeks and rustles.... I feel a presence beside me and slightly behind me. I turn around startled .But no! Nothing! ...Shades!!

And then when I sit in the car going home for the holidays....the hour late because of a puncture and road blocks....the car meandering through fields and over culverts....the headlights picking out the bushes on either side, looking as though they had just had time to change into bushes form whatever form they'd been assuming in the dark. I look back thinking to catch them in the act of changing back into..... what??..... Gnomes? Goblins? Witches?...But the dark conspire to hide them and keeps their secret from prying eyes.

And when home is reached its past midnight and too tired for pleasantries. I only want to crawl into bed. But I just can't resist standing at the window for a few minutes to take in the breathtaking loveliness of a moonlit countryside-a soothing balm to my town weary eyes. But today, the tall trees in the vast grounds trailing their creepers and vines seem solemn and sinister, silently soaking in the moonlight, with not a breath of air to stir a leaf. The fields beyond , stretching as far as the eye could see, lay sleeping as though with one ear cocked like a dog, and the dark mountains seem to loom over the whole scene menacingly. A midnight owl gives a sudden hoot and in the stillness it makes me jump. A lazy breeze comes out of nowhere to rustle the leaves and out of the corner of my eyes I see a tall white-clad lissome beauty with dark luxuriant tresses unbound beckoning me from a coppice!! For a minute I stand petrified, my heart hammering against my ribs. Then I see that it's only a long banana leaf set against some creepers. But was it?? You never know in such pristine surroundings where myth and reality play hide and seek. I hastily retreat to the safety of the bed and bury myself in my blankets.

Shades!!..always tantalizing and giving me the slip at the last minute....What are they??? Manifestations of another world? Or things of this world of ours? Things that can change form and shape when no conscious mind observes them?? I live for the day I can catch them out at their morphing.

THE ILL BEHAV

THE ILL BEHAVED WAVE-FUNCTION

[It's now been proved that particles are not just particles but they are also waves. Smaller the particle greater is the wave character, so that, the tiniest particles like electrons in atoms behave somewhat like light waves. To describe a wave and its properties in mathematics we make use of a short hand and this is called a wave function-it tells you all that you wanted to know about the particle and it's wave. So you see a wave function is not a walking talking physical entity that it can behave well or ill –the epithet only refers to whether it is successful or not in describing the properties of the wave]

"Every state of a particle is associated with a wave function" droned the teacher in a dull monotone. L stifled a yawn, trying vainly to keep her eyes open. She cursed herself for the hundredth time for her movie addiction. But, for God's sake, it was Titanic on Star Movies last night! Even now her eyes filled with tears at the thought of poor dear Leonardo sinking into the icy sea .So poignant! And she had seen the movie so many times..........

".......should be well behaved. Otherwise it is not acceptable." The teacher's voice suddenly penetrated her conciousness.She rubbed her eyes and looked about her.

No, it was not the English class, but the chemistry class. But what was this about somebody being well behaved? Surely not her?

"Who's well behaved ma'am?"

"Oh! I believe our sleeping beauty has come back to us after all. What was it last night? Titanic?"

"How did you know ma'am?"

"Sixth Sense"

"But who should be well behaved ma'am?

"Our old friend the wave function"

"You were saying ma'am, that every particle should be associated with a wave function"

"Ha! So you weren't entirely asleep"

"But, ma'am is there a wave function associated with me?"

"You are too big a particle for your wave properties to be apparent"

"But, ma'am, we are made up of electrons, protons and neutrons, and they are all associated with wave functions. So there could be one wave function for our mental state and another one for our physical state, don't you think ma'am?"

"Oh! So you would shift the blame for your mental state to your wave function would you?"

Ma'am, suppose the wave function is not well behaved?"

"Well, if it isn't well behaved it cannot be accepted as a wave function you silly girl"

"But you told us that some things that are quantum mechanically forbidden do take place, only, the probability is less. So maybe a person's wave function is ill-behaved, which is why he is cruel or selfish or ill-behaved?"

"I now know that your wave function is perfectly idiotic, otherwise, you wouldn't be asking such stupid questions. Sit down this minute. Not another word out of you again."

"That's what they did to Einstein," L muttered under her breath, "But they couldn't suppress him"

"I could suppress you quite easily," said ma'am in a silky smooth voice which was somehow infinitely more menacing. Her impositions were legendary, never less than 100, and she was quite ruthless. L subsided in her place reflecting on this unjust world and the wave function of her mental state promptly switched over to the dreaming mode

MY RAIN

Jyolsna. B (My Daughter)
MY RAIN

Rain
like a sweet symphony
like a melodious Ghazhal
replenishing my arid heart
filling it with a rainbow

Rain
like a soothing lullaby
like a haunting cry at night
lulling me to sleep
waking me up with rude patterings

Rain
like a soulful tune
like a divine finger
laid upon my heart
beating in sync with my rhythm

Rain
like a rousing lyric
like a lover's warm caress
drenching me in colours
murmuring sweet nothings
as I ecstatically burs into a fountain
embracing you, becoming one with you

Rain
Like a lonely cry at night
Like the vacuum beside my bed
Black as my tears
Raging in vacant fury
Lashing out at nothing vainly
Trying to fill the void
With a thousand unsaid words

Rain
Like a blind broken song
Like a warm painless death
In my sad sleepless nights
Old, desolate, weary
Trickling away, fading away
Like the flowers and candles upon my grave

Rain
Like the sun in my dreams at night
Like the moon in my dreams of day
Drawing me out, moving me to tears
Inspiring me with a verse
And I aspire to heaven
With my
Feet in chains.

RELAAAX...ZZZ...ING

OH..UH..Sitting down at long last. I've been on my feet since 6 in the morning—even had my breakfast standing up! Late as usual and rushed as usual! Now at last I'm in the bus to college. I take a few long, deep breaths and look at the view from the window (for of course I am in a window seat!). I get bored almost immediately—the same old places I've been seeing for more than 30 years. Bye and bye the conductor comes along and I take my ticket. He goes away grumbling about old women who never have any change (hair not dyed—grey all over—been putting it off and putting it off for 2 weeks now). Well, with that hurdle out of the way, I calculate that I will get a clear 40 minutes to catch up on my beauty sleep. Accordingly I close my eyes and lean back on the head rest. Hardly had my head touched the head rest than the bus gives a sudden jolt and I am thrown forward, specs and all, and almost hit the front seat. If that had happened my specs would have been shattered and the shards of glass would have pierced my eyes. My heart is racing fit to jump out of the ribcage. I lean back and try to calm myself.

It's then that I remember an article in the New Indian Express about utilizing your time during the daily commute. The writer had enumerated the eight-fold path—repeat affirmations, find a solution, look at people and study them, listen to an audio book, make plans, meditate, learn a foreign language or relax your body, instead of playing with your Smartphone (or with any phone, for that matter), reading books or listening to music. Though, I couldn't figure why listening to an audio book should be superior to reading a printed book.

When I thought of all the alternatives, I liked the idea of relaxing the best. I had learnt the relaxation technique during our yoga classes in college, in the days when the UGC timings were strictly imposed. I still had 30 minutes. So I closed my eyes and started with the deep breathing, counting down from 10. The next step was to start relaxing your body from the feet up, visualizing that part of the body. You would start with the right foot I suppose? Must be, because you always want to start right, right? Ok. So, I started with the right leg. Right leg from toes to knee relaaaaxx. Next, left leg from toes to knee relaaax. Then, from knees to hip for both the legs. Then, torso from hips to the neck relaaaax... at this time you have to imagine stroking your internal organs too so they would also relax.

Suddenly my eyes flew wide open...the bus was stopped at the traffic signal at Malapparamba. I hastily gather up my scattered bags and jump out before the lights change. What had happened? The last I remembered, I had been doing the relaxation!

Well, I had obviously forgotten what invariably happened during 'savasana' in the yoga class—somebody always had to prod me awake! So in the end it was Plan A that worked and not Plan B! Thank God I did not reach Paropady or Maikunnu—it had happened many times before! And on that positive note I hurried to the auto stand for the last leg of the journey.

B. Lakshmi Devi,
Associate Prof. of Chemistry

STOP DYEING AND START LIVING

No it's not about dying
As in not living or suicide
You don't get rid of me that easily
Intend to live to ripe old age

It's about tinting your hair
To keep old age at bay
"Your face looks young, so why
Do you go about looking so grey?"

"Black, brown, burgundy---list's endless
To tempt your every mood
(Even pink like Tonks* ? Wish I were she)
The mind is literally boggled"

But once you are in, it's for keeps
The new look lasts four weeks, max
For the new hair not knowing it's supposed
to be colored
Turns up in the original grey

And then it's back to the Smelly Portions
And an hour of your life gone waste
Which, else, could have been gainfully spent

At TV or chatting or sleep
So, join me yea young – oldies
Let's grow old gracefully
And when tempted sorely, let's chant the mantra
"Stop dyeing and start living"
(* the character in Harry Potter novels who could change her hair color just by sheer will power)

A Lazy Midsummer Afternoon—A Rare Communion

'Tis sweet to hold communion
With Nature true and wild,
And feel the thrill of gladness
She breathes upon her child
--Jared Barhite-- Communion With Nature

The rain came down in torrents –a gallon to a drop. It flowed down the terraces in miniature waterfalls, carrying the flame coloured flowers of the May Queen, tearing the red carpet to tatters, and roared off down an unknown drain. The girl walking on the main driveway seemed to have no feet, and seemed to glide along—her feet hidden by the spray as the raindrops hit the tarred surface of the road. Thunder rumbled overhead. Suddenly there was a blinding flash, followed almost immediately by an ear-splitting crash. It startled the students who had been too intent on their exams to notice anything.

It had been a quiet afternoon – almost too quiet it would seem—when I had come to take up the invigilation duty. It was during the summer 'holidays' and the usual hustle and bustle was missing. There were only 5 girls writing the exam that day and two invigilators were way too superfluous. So… there we were-two of us teachers with nothing to do, and three long hours to while away. I stood in the doorway enjoying the breeze. The May Flower trees were in full bloom, their orange-red flowers making an entrancingly delicate tracery against the pale blue sky. The ground was strewn with the flowers like a red carpet spread out to welcome all comers. I let the silence and the beauty sink into my very soul rejuvenating it.

It was then that the sky had started darkening – imperceptibly at first then getting darker by the minute. Suddenly a cold wind swept through the class room tossing the papers about and the rain followed soon after.

The light and sound show lasted all of half an hour. It stopped as suddenly as it had started and the sun was shining just as though it was business as usual and the storm had never happened. It steamed away the moisture wherever it touched seeking to remove the last traces. But, the rain had brought a welcome surcease to the burning heat, settling the dust and leaving the air bright and clear.

I took a deep breath of the intoxicating wet-earth scent. The storm had chased away the mid afternoon drowsiness and I felt invigorated. Storms do that to me. They are exhilarating—especially if its after dark with the power supply cut off—removing the last barrier between me and the primeval fury of nature unleashed. The raw power of the wind, rain, thunder and lightning just surge through me—atonement (at-one-ment) pure and complete.

(Though sometimes it's tinged with a twinge of guilt when I think of my servant's home where the water is likely to come in, like an uninvited guest).

Away from the tumult of motor and mill
I want to be care-free; I want to be still!
I'm weary of doing things; weary of words
I want to be one with the blossoms and birds. *Edgar A. Guest*

Nature in her more benign and sublime moods too touch my heart strings to evoke a sweet and haunting melody. Like the Sunday afternoons in the height of summer when, well fed and content, I lie down for the well earned rest. Outside the sun is blazing hot. But in my room, under the shade of the fragrant jasmine tree, it's quiet and cool. I watch the leaves casting shifting shadows on the glass as they are ruffled by the light breeze and a feeling of contentment steals over my senses lulling me into a half sleep. Or, the time when I am rushing to college in an auto on a dreary morning, late as usual. The sky is overcast threatening rain. Suddenly a single ray of sunlight bursts through a gap in the clouds, illuminating a laden 'konna' tree, turning it into a poem in pure gold. It's only the very briefest of glimpses as the auto speeds by, but for a moment the veil was drawn back, and I glimpsed the face of the creator. Cut to another locale—this one an air-conditioned forest. We were on a one day picnic, my students and I. The trees overhead seemed almost to meet and we walked through a cool verdant tunnel, all our cares and all our weariness forgotten in such pristine surroundings, when a turn brings us face to face with a brook with ice cold water, gurgling over rocks and huge boulders, the bed strewn with white 'vellaramkallu'(white granite stones)— beautiful beyond compare. Or, evenings at my favorite Krishna temple, atop a hillock, where I can look out over the small pond, the open sky a riot of sunset colors, the lamps all lit and the pooja bells tinkling, inducing a prayerful mood, recharging the spent spirit and the weary soul. Or the majestic harvest moon, rising over the rooftops, solemn and mysterious. Its one of the few times when I have wished for a power failure and bandh— to blot out the ever present reminders of civilization that marred the sublime moment. All and each have been to me a rapture and an ecstasy, that none of the modern aids to entertainment can hope to match.

The ringing of the bell recalled me to my duties. The brief communion with nature—the storm—I stored in my heart, along with all the other vignettes, to sooth a 'vacant or a pensive mood' with 'tranquil restoration'.

THE BIRTHING

It was midnight and the clock did chime
Twelve weary notes into the dreary night
And called forth the restless spirit
From its slumberless grave

One moment

Of madness

The dagger

Buried

To the hilt

In his

Heart

Surcease?

From sorrow?

For ever?

No! Never!

For the raging thirst for the ruby red wine
Drove her lips to the wound, as his curse became hers
And the penultimate moment before eternity claimed her
She knew she was doomed, from the gleam in his eyes

www.ingramcontent.com/pod-product-compliance
Lightning Source LLC
LaVergne TN
LVHW050429160726
843469LV00041B/1292

* 9 7 8 9 3 5 4 3 8 1 0 0 3 *